This Topsy and Tim
book belongs to

Maya Kad.

Topsy + Tim

go to hospital

Jean and Gareth Adamson

Ladybird

Published by Ladybird Books Ltd
80 Strand London WC2R 0RL
A Penguin (UK) Company

5 7 9 10 8 6

Printed in Italy

Tim was going to hospital.
He had fallen out of a tree
and bumped his head.
Topsy and Mummy helped Tim
to pack the things he would need
in hospital.

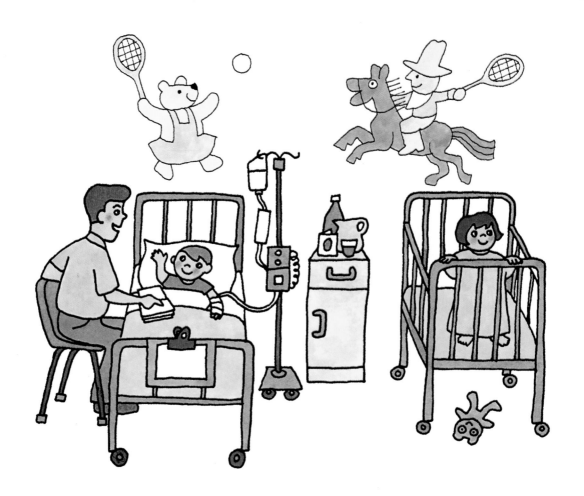

The hospital was very big,
with bedrooms called wards.
One ward had funny pictures
on the walls.
'This must be the children's ward,'
said Mummy.
A nurse called Sister helped Tim
put his things away in his own
special locker.

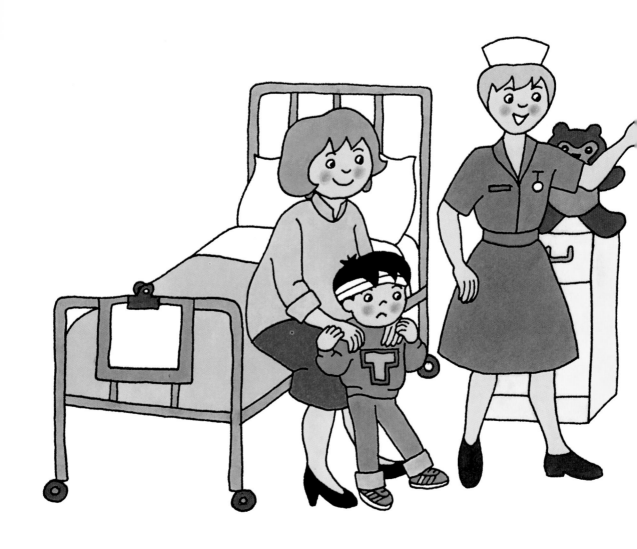

'The porter will take you to be
photographed in a minute,' said Sister.
'It will be an X-ray photograph—
the kind that shows what you
look like inside.'

The porter came,
pushing a big
wheelchair for Tim
to sit in.
'Can Mummy come
too?' asked Tim.
'Of course she can,'
said Sister.

It was a long way to the X-ray room.
Tim enjoyed his wheelchair ride.

He saw another porter pushing a
little girl along. She waved to Tim
as they passed.

The lady who worked the X-ray camera stood behind a screen. She could see Tim through a little window.

Mummy stayed with Tim but she
had to wear a special apron.
The X-ray photograph was soon taken.

After lunch, the children went to bed.
Mummy tucked Tim in.
'Now I must go home to look after
Topsy,' she said. 'But don't worry,
I'll soon be back.'

'Bring Topsy with you,' said Tim.
'I will,' said Mummy, but Tim
didn't hear. He was already
fast asleep.

Topsy brought her best jigsaw puzzle
when she came to see Tim in hospital.
She thought he would like to play
with it in bed.

Tim was not in bed. He was playing with the other children.

He took Topsy to meet his new friends.

On the way home, Topsy told Mummy
she had a pain—but she was not sure
where it was. Mummy did not
believe her.
'I want to go to hospital too,'
said Topsy.

'Cheer up, Topsy,' said Dad, when
he came home from work. 'I've brought
a surprise present for you.'

The surprise present was a medical set with a syringe, a stethoscope and a thermometer.

When Topsy came home from school
next day, she found Tim waiting
for her.
'Mummy brought me home,' said Tim.
'My head's all right now.'

Soon every toy in the house was in
Topsy and Tim's children's hospital.